The Tudor Trump

T0364505

Written and illustrated by Nadine Cowan

Collins

Chapter 1

Aniyah savoured the taste of the fried sweet dough she was sharing with her cousin EJ and their friend Olivia. It was called a festival – one of her favourite snacks from Jamaica. The lunch-time rush at Blue Mahoes, Aniyah and EJ's family restaurant, was over and now they wanted to play their favourite board game.

The Ludi board had brightly coloured squares and painted African masks in the centre. There was an engraving which read:

Roll double six, or double three,
let's learn about your history.

This wasn't just any game. Whenever they played, something amazing happened!

Olivia shook the dice and moved her counter.

"I went on a boat tour on the Thames and visited the London Eye yesterday," Olivia said. "I saw the restaurant from up there, so I waved to you both!"

Before she could say any more, EJ rolled double three. Suddenly, the board illuminated like a fluorescent bulb. The table shook and a tornado that formed a wormhole pulled the children in.

Aniyah and Olivia found themselves in a courtyard. Aniyah felt as though a snake had wrapped itself tightly around her waist. She looked down and saw that she was wearing a tight bodice over a gown and linen smock. A small drawstring bag hung from her belt.

"We look like princesses!" Olivia said. "I wonder where we are?"

They could hear music and cheering in the distance.

Aniyah wrinkled her nose.

"Wherever we are, it stinks! Where's EJ?"

"He can't be far –" Olivia began, when someone barged into her.

Paper with drawings on fluttered around them, and coloured chalks and black ink spilled to the ground.

"I beg your pardon!" a man exclaimed, as the girls helped him pick up his things.

"Are you a painter?" Olivia asked, handing him some paper.

"Thank you, yes! I was gathering inspiration for the tournament roll and wasn't looking where I was going."

"There's to be a joust in London, in honour of the birth of King Henry VIII's son, and I've been commissioned to paint the tournament. 1511 will go down in history!" replied the painter, before rushing off.

"1511!" gasped Aniyah.

"Henry VIII!" Olivia said at the same time. "No way!"

"What's a joust?" Aniyah said.

"No idea!" Olivia replied. "Maybe it's something to do with the decorations."

The girls looked down at the ground. The black ink the artist had dropped had formed a big, gooey puddle.

"What a mess," said Olivia.

Just then, a dark shadow loomed over them. When they turned round, they saw a figure in full armour.
The girls gulped.

Chapter 2

Laughter erupted from the helmet as the visor was lifted. It was EJ!

"You should've seen your faces! This is way cooler than what I arrived in. I found it in that palace over there," EJ pointed.

Suddenly, a man holding something wrapped in cloth shoved past them.

"That's the second person!" Aniyah grumbled.

A voice cried out, "THIEF! STOP HIM!" and a man wearing an ornate turban stopped to catch his breath beside them.

"What did he take?" asked EJ.

"My trumpet!" the man gasped. "I only rested it for a moment. I'm John; I'm a musician of the court and I need that trumpet for today's festivities."

"Look!" Olivia pointed to the black ink on the ground.

"It's the thief's footprints!" Aniyah's face lit up. "We can follow them and help you get your trumpet back."

"Thank you. We've got to be quick!" said John. "I can't be late."

They all looked at EJ in his heavy armour.

EJ sighed. "I'll go and change."

They left the armour behind some crates and followed the inky footprints, dodging through the crowds.

"These footprints should lead us straight to the –" EJ's jaw dropped, and the girls could see why. There was a huge celebration ahead, and the footprints faded into the crowd.

"We'll never find him here!" said Aniyah.

"There's another way out of Westminster. The thief may be heading for the wharf," John replied.

"Westminster? It looks so different; I rode the number 38 bus here yesterday!" said Olivia.

"I wish we could jump on the 38 right now!" huffed Aniyah.

The stench grew stronger as they clambered down some steps to a river.

"This must be the Thames," said Olivia.

"Look!" said EJ. "It's another footprint."

There was a boat heading towards a bridge.
Olivia squinted.

"That's the man who ran past us."

The riverbank was lined with watermen waiting to ferry people across the river.

"Where's that boat heading?" John asked them.

"The man asked to go to Venours Wharf," came the reply.

"Can you take us there?" asked John.

The waterman looked at John's luxurious clothing. "Tuppence each."

"Each!?" John cried.

"Take it or leave it," the waterman replied.

John peered inside his little black purse and emptied the contents.

"Welcome aboard," sang the waterman.

The small boat pulled away from the wharf as the waterman rowed against the tide. He navigated past the other boats sailing towards Westminster from Southwark.

Suddenly, a ferocious wave came crashing against the boat. Everyone gripped the sides tightly. The boat began to tip sideways, and water crept inside.

Chapter 3

The waterman heaved the oars with all his might, then let out a raspy laugh.

"The Thames won't bite; it's just saying hello."

Olivia, Aniyah and EJ couldn't believe how different London looked from the river. There was no London Eye, no Big Ben and only one bridge.

"Is it far?" EJ asked John.

"No, but it's quicker to travel by boat," John explained. "I've not seen you at the palace before. London can be a dangerous place; there are lots of pickpockets. The poor have little money and can't afford to clothe or feed themselves. I'm fortunate enough to have a highly respected job that pays well."

"What's it like being a court musician?" Olivia asked John.

"No two days are the same. I get to travel and attend grand banquets. I also get to stay in places most could only dream of, but the hours are long. I played the trumpet in yesterday's procession to Westminster while on horseback. If I don't get my trumpet back, I'll lose my job."

When the waterman pulled up beside Venours Wharf, everyone clambered out, thankful that they hadn't been gobbled up by the river.

Aniyah pointed to a wet, murky footprint. "The thief must've washed the ink off in the river."

They followed the wet footprints, but they soon disappeared.

"This road leads to Cheapside, and that's where I think a thief would go to sell my trumpet," John said.

Cheapside was lined with shops, stalls and taverns.

EJ looked around. “It’s not as fancy as Westminster.”

As they drew near, they heard cheering and laughing. People were dancing to the notes of a pipe mingled in with the sound of sellers bartering goods.

“I fear the thief will be long gone, but we may find my trumpet,” said John.

Chapter 4

"Is that it?" Olivia beckoned them over to a shop display where there was a gleaming trumpet, its painted silk banner draped down below.

"Yes!" John cried. He grabbed it.

"I paid a heavy price for that," the shopkeeper said. "I'll accept nothing less than 35 shillings!"

"I spent all the money I had with me on the boat ride," cried John.

Aniyah remembered her leather purse. When she opened it, she found some shiny jewellery and coins. She pulled the jewellery out and held it in the palm of her hand.

"That jewellery is worth a pretty penny," said the shopkeeper.

"You can have it in exchange for the trumpet!" Aniyah said excitedly. "I have enough coins for a boat ride back, too."

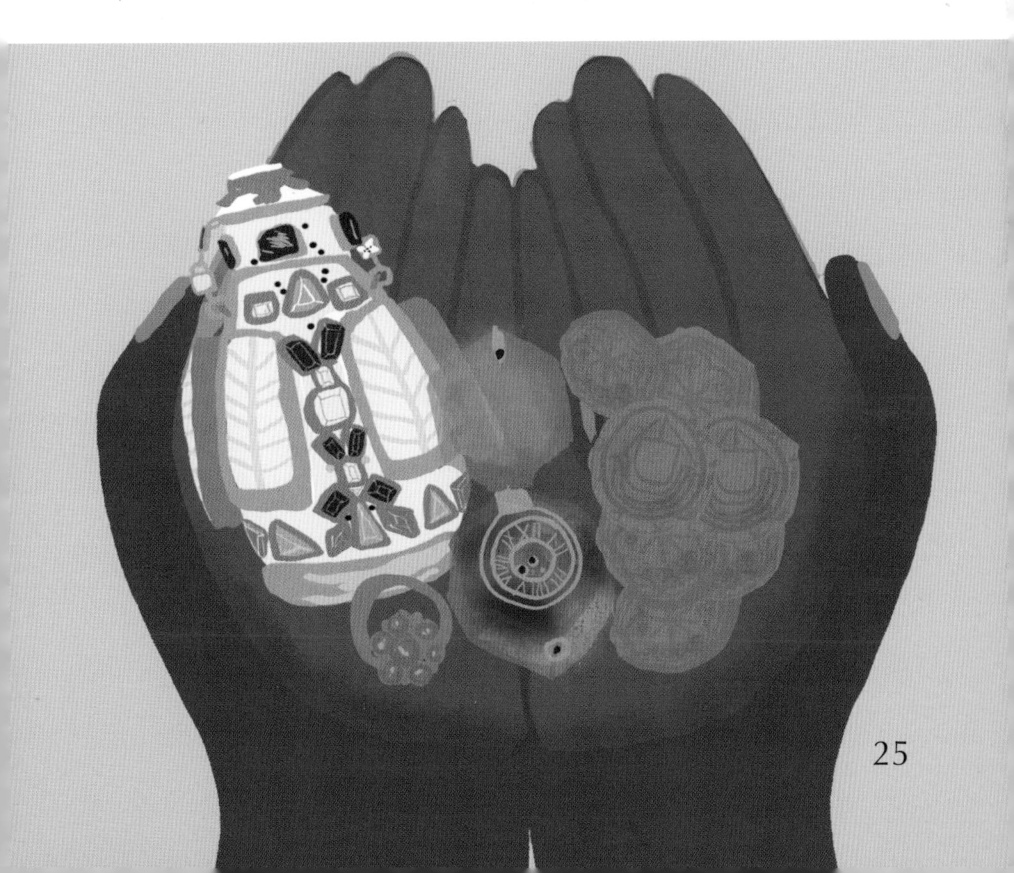

After another choppy boat ride, the children walked to Westminster Palace with John.

"I am most grateful for your assistance," John said, as he mounted his horse. "I must go now but do stay for the joust."

Olivia and Aniyah stroked the horse's shiny mane before John rode away.

The children found a space at the front in the tiltyard and were mesmerised by John's trumpet solo. When John had finished, he waved to the children before continuing with the other trumpeters.

The trumpets sounded once more as knights on horseback came galloping out into the yard.

"This must be what a joust is!" said Aniyah.

The crowd erupted into a cheer when Henry VIII appeared. He made a grand gesture to the queen before he rode over to face his opponent. The jousters lowered their visors and began to charge. But just as the king raised his lance, a cloud of smoke appeared and a tornado that formed a wormhole pulled the children in.

They were back in the restaurant!

"Just as it was getting good!" said EJ.

"I'm glad to get away from that awful smell!" Aniyah said, taking a deep breath.

"Whose turn is it to roll the dice?" asked Olivia, as they gathered around the board once more.

Follow the footprints

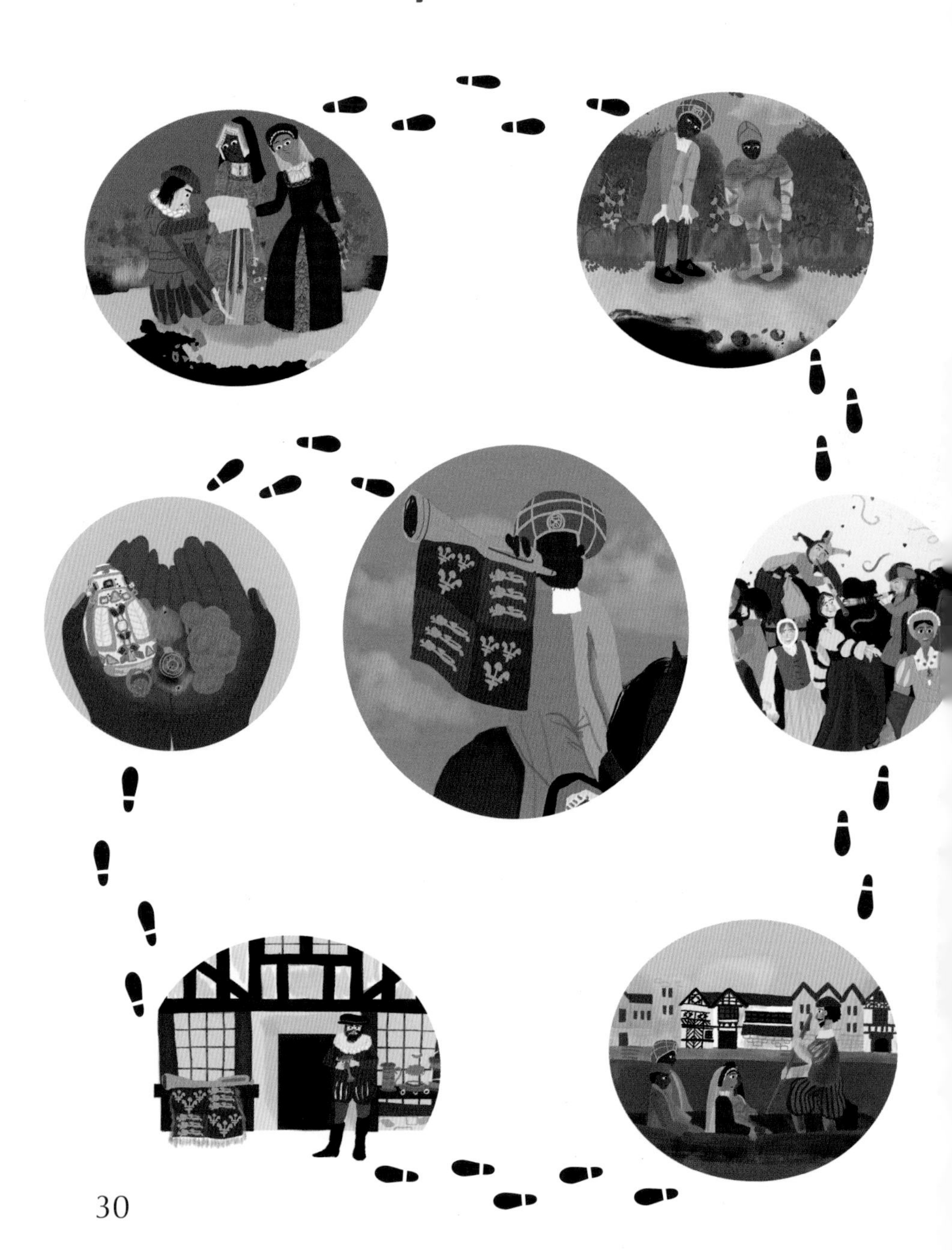

Real people

John Blanke

John Blanke was a royal trumpeter at the court of King Henry VIII. In 1511, he played during a two-day celebration to mark the birth of Henry's son. We don't know much about John, but we do know he asked the king for a pay rise, and he got it!

Ideas for reading

Written by Gill Matthews
Primary Literacy Consultant

Reading objectives:

- check that the text makes sense to them, discuss their understanding and explaining the meaning of words in context
- ask questions to improve their understanding of a text
- participate in discussion about books, taking turns and listening to what others say

Spoken language objectives:

- ask relevant questions to extend their understanding and knowledge
- maintain attention and participate actively in collaborative conversations, staying on topic and initiating and responding to comments
- participate in discussions, presentations, performances, role play, improvisations and debates

Curriculum links: History: a study of an aspect or theme in British history that extends pupils' chronological knowledge beyond 1066

Interest words: erupted, shoved, ornate, gasped, celebration

Build a context for reading

- Show children the front cover and read the title. Ask what the title means to them. Explore their knowledge of Tudor times.
- Read the back-cover blurb. Ask what they think will happen in this story.

Understand and apply reading strategies

- Read pp2–5 aloud, using appropriate expression. Ask the children to summarise what has happened in the story opening. Discuss the characters who have been introduced.
- Ask children to read pp6–9, again using appropriate expression. Establish where and when the characters have found themselves.
- Explain that the tournament roll is a series of painted pictures showing the events that were held to celebrate the birth of Henry VIII's son.
- Ask children what they think a tournament is and what a joust is.
- Discuss how the girls are feeling at the end of the chapter.
- Give children the opportunity to read the rest of the story.